CAFÉ PASSION:

A Java Romance

By

Elle Bell

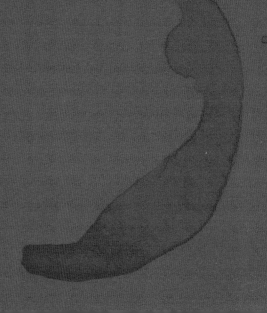

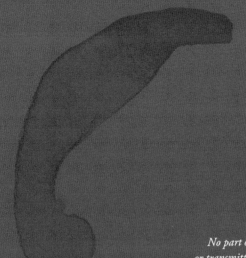

AuthorHouse™ LLC
1663 Liberty Drive
Bloomington, IN 47403
www.authorhouse.com
Phone: 1-800-839-8640

Published by AuthorHouse 08/30/2013

ISBN: 978-1-4918-0925-9 (sc)
978-1-4918-0926-6 (e)

Library of Congress Control Number: 2013914623

authorhouse®

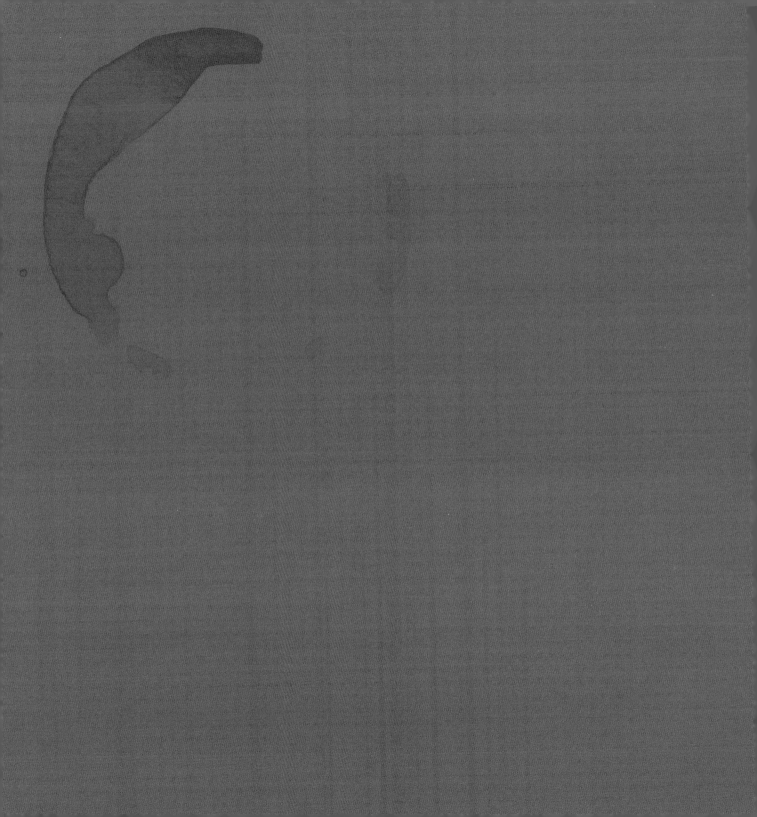

PROLOGUE

Coffee is a passion for many of you who are paging through my book today. Where would we be without our coffee? I'm not sure where I would be without mine. This realization occurred to me during an especially tumultuous time in my life. I felt lost, alone, abandoned and geographically in a place I had never been before. I have never been consistent with anything; my life was about constant change. Except coffee. Coffee was always there. Coffee always made me feel warm, at home and loved – even when I was alone and far away from home. So, every morning it was coffee and me against the whole world! Coffee inspired me to stay positive, to move forward and find my passion. I hope your love of coffee, together with this book, inspires you to find yours. Here we are, bonded on common grounds!

ACKNOWLEDGEMENTS

My husband Philip, who has always believed in me, made this book possible. He is my sanity, my strength and my support. Thank you for being such a marvelous and devoted husband!

Thank you to my brilliant kids, who quickly learned not to bring up complicated subjects in the morning until at least the second cup. Much love to my sister in law, Sarah, and black coffee Jennie – whose java passion sparked my obsession. A zillion thanks to all my family and friends for their love, support and encouragement.

Much of the amazing photo art displayed on these pages are the creation of my brilliant and talented niece, Amber. Contact information for professional referrals:

ap-photography @ hotmail.com

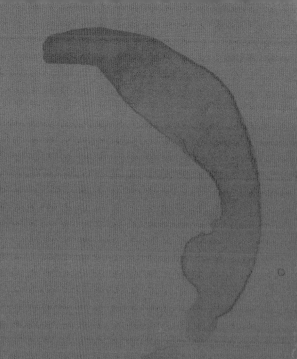

For my husband and children.

TABLE OF CONTENTS

Love, Wisdom, Addiction 1

The Affair 19

The Essence of Life 31

Love
Wisdom
Addiction

~ Some of the longest and dreaded times for the two of us are at night when we are apart. How do you know if it is coffee love you crave? You know you are in love with coffee when you cannot wait to get that sleeping thing over with to **attack** another new day fueled by Starbucks® Espresso roast! Yea, baby!

~ It's exactly like enjoying a harmonious and magnificently brilliant symphony when listening to the magic coffee pot brew its miraculous and potent elixir...

~ At the epicenter of true thankfulness is a thought to ponder. This beautiful contemplation will warm the heart and radiate right down to icy little toes: imagine hot, rich and spiced fresh brewed Starbucks® Thanksgiving blend coffee.... I can almost smell it... Begin with this, and you will realize there are so many reasons to be thankful, every day...

~ There's an old Chinese proverb that says, "The journey of a thousand miles begins with a single step". As this dense and sleepy fog begins to lift, these are the motivating words that get me to the coffee pot... Even though I do not think that is what the old Chinese guy meant when he said it...

~ What exactly is a coffee ninja? A coffee ninja is an undercover ninja, and is usually the last person you would expect. It is a person who has pledged allegiance to coffee, and lives by the coffee code. Usually this person is under disguise, and is often clumsy to hide their true identity- but whose powers and stealth come alive when injected with the lifeblood: coffee. Picture this: currently I have a blow dryer in one hand, and a mug of coffee in the other. The question must be asked, how is it at all possible to write out this entry? Telepathically, of course- because that's how coffee ninjas get things done!

~ Monday Mantra: Kick off your week on a positive note. Repeat after me: "Hello and good morning Monday! Woo hoo!! What a great and fantastic day to be alive!" Without hesitation - immediately follow up these words with a half pot of Starbucks® Espresso roast coffee. The week is started right!

~ Have you ever turned around and **poof** your cup of coffee is empty? I have a theory: Everybody has heard of garden gnomes, but is there such a thing as a coffee gnome? I think so. If people can believe in Sasquatch, there HAS to be coffee gnomes...How else can I possibly go through so many pots of coffee each and every day? These silent, sneaky and extraordinarily jubilant miniature creatures, I believe, are responsible for the daily occurrences of missing cups of coffee around the globe. Be camera ready, and capture one!

~ If I was stranded on a deserted island and could only have one thing, I know what I would choose. The latest edition of "The Ultimate Coffee Ninja Survival Manual: Stranded on a Deserted Island Edition". Mostly, because Chapter 8 is about growing your own coffee right on the beach and that is all anybody needs to survive. How bad could being stranded on a deserted island be if you have coffee? I mean, really?

~ Some people wait for once a year to vacation on a cruise liner at some distant, glorious destination. My choice is to take an imagination vacation every morning. What, you ask, is my favorite port of call? You guessed it- the coffeepot in the kitchen... Although on occasion unseen forces create potential roadblocks between me and true bliss. Today, as I lay in bed, there's mutiny on the ship between my coffee desire and these lazy bones!

~ *I think animals should know the goodness of coffee, too. I have been thinking- and I don't think it would be difficult or complicated at all. All we do is get farmers to replace plain old ordinary salt lick blocks for cows- with salted "caramel espresso" lick blocks. Perhaps we will start a salted caramel coffee flavored milk phenomenon!*

~ *Be thankful for every thing, every day. Start out each morning being thankful for the opportunity to wake with breath in your lungs, vision in your eyes, health in your body, and the potential for coffee rushing through your veins.*

~ *Doesn't it just feel great to sleep in? (For some of you out there who are new parents – you will remember what that is like, some day – I promise.) It just feels so refreshing; my body feels so alive! Take note that during this rare occurrence, you don't even need coffee on these mornings! Ha, kidding! I was just checking to see if any of you kids out there were paying attention. Go ahead, indulge. It feels a lot like a cherry sitting on top of the perfect sundae with all that sleep under your belt, doesn't it?*

~ *I find myself sleepily driving through the dismal gray, all of the world's colors dripping into one. I feel empty, passionless. Driving on what seems to be an endlessly winding road... In the distance is the faint, comfortable glow... and that's when I saw her; a beacon of light in the dreary darkness, a vision of beauty like none other... Long flowing hair, righteous crown and her captivating aroma drew me to her. Oh, lady on the Starbucks® sign,*
I love you.

~ *Remembering a time when I moved to the country, to be with the open sky, peaceful breeze, whistling trees and serenading wildlife that I'd been dreaming of for so very, very long. Even though I dreaded packing up my whole life, moving wasn't hard to do with coffee. Coffee helped me bubble wrap my breakables, and pack everything into the van. We did everything together. I remember my moving friends watching as I buckled coffeepot's safety belt as he rode shot gun. They could have had the front seat, but they didn't call it first. Still makes me laugh to think about it...*

~ *Don't you just gotta love kids? Mine set up the coffeepot for me; the French Roast was so, so very dark that as I drank it, my eyes began to water. On a lighter note, I suddenly have a taste for toasted baguettes and an urge to say, "Bonjour! Je m'appelle Danielle. Je suis très heureux de faire votre connaissance! Oh, by the way, parler-vouz francais?"*

~ Did you ever lay down in bed and swear you just closed your eyes and **!!!BAM!!!**
It's morning? You have the choice to look at it one of two ways:
#1: The coffee cup half empty - I am not really sure what this one would be, although it
may be some type of complaint about the morning coming too quickly. My question would
be, who could complain about morning when it's time for coffee?
 # 2: The coffee cup is half full - Last night was the shortest wait EVER to make coffee
this morning! Woo hoo! Let's dance! **shakes it**

~ Me -n- coffee, sitting in a tree, k-i-s-s-i-n-g... Be unashamed of coffee love. Climb
trees together – experience life, don't let others keep you apart – love coffee unabashedly
and completely... get caught k-i-s-s-i-n-g in a tree...

~ Have you hugged your coffee today? I did, mine hugged me back... Try it, you will
see... Feel the love...

~ A very important recipe to enjoy a little smidge of paradise on earth: Join curly,
swirled ribbons of deep, rich espresso with hot, sweet, foamy steamed milk- add a splash
of decadent amber colored English toffee syrup and...Viola! ...Homemade nirvana!

~ Some say dance like nobody is watching... Well, let's sing like nobody is listening! Let's pretend we are far away in the mountains with fields of flowers all around us – miles from where anyone can hear! Use your coffee cup as a microphone and really give it all you got!! EVERYBODY ♀♂ SING WITH ME! ♪Oh what a beautiful morning! ☼ Oh what a beautiful day! ♪ Every thing's brighter and better! ♪ ☼ With espresso roast♪ coming my way! ♪

~ Almost walked out the door for work today without my coffee, which is actually the exact equivalent of leaving the house without pants on. Never a good idea... Not ever.

~ I am staying in a hotel away from home, vacationing. I can't help but notice everyone who walks by my room says, "WOW! That coffee smells soooo good!" ...and I wonder - why is it they are noticing? Doesn't everyone travel with their Espresso roast? Why would anyone not bring along their coffee to share such wonderful vacation memories? This year, let your coffee have the beach lounge chair next to you as you sun at the pool. Purchase the photo of the two of you sitting wide eyed next to each other, hair blown back on the craziest roller coaster....
Cherish these special moments together.

~ Gazing lovingly at my coffee, while he is looking back at me. What an overwhelming excitement just to be together! I feel like I am 5 years old, it's Christmas morning and Santa pulled exactly what I wanted out of his red, velvet toy sack... feels good to be a kid again.

~ *I like to play "memory games" each day – I tell myself it will help to keep my mind sharp. This game usually consists of walking around the house with my cup of coffee and trying to remember where I left it when I realize I don't have it anymore. Since I have moved into a teeny tiny house I am the master of my mega memory coffee game.*

~ *Just as every wise man passes down to his son to never pee into the wind, this exact same concept becomes absolute wisdom when dumping a full travel mug of old coffee from a moving vehicle. Just don't do it.*
Trust me.

~ *Did you ever get that sense of impending doom? I had it all morning. I was so foggy, I couldn't figure it out. Then I finally realized, I think I may have done something illegal...I drove to work entirely without having had a single drop of coffee. (I am discovering this may also explain why some of my clothing is on inside out... again)*

~ *It's the middle of the day and the birds are shining and the sun is singing...Is there ever a wrong time for coffee? I don't think so, and if birds are shining and the sun is singing perhaps it should be made a serious priority.*

~ *Coffee isn't just something to enjoy, and it's not only a state of mind, I think of it as more of a lifestyle. What coffee lover would not base the purchase of a vehicle solely on coffee cup accessibility? Or consider the purchase of their home based on the counter space and centrally located placement of their coffee pot? Or plan a garden based on how it is viewed from the coffee nook of your home? This all makes sense to me. One day at work, I shared with a friend these basic coffee lifestyle principles. After sharing my thoughts, my friend suggested perhaps I should look into rehab for coffee addicts. I just laughed, and then proceeded to go back to my office to finish off the evidence...*

~ *I dream of creating my own brand new coffee blend: I imagine it to be dark and smooth with stealthy and mysterious undertones. It shall be called "Night Ninja Blend" coffee. Many people do not know the ways of the coffee ninja, it's such a secretive society. One random fact I could share with you without sabotaging the coffee ninja culture, is coffee was originated as the preferred drink of coffee ninjas since 1973-ish.*

~ Shuffling down the hall from the bedroom like the living dead, I manage to squeak out a rusty moan to my kids passing by. Joints stiff and achy, I slowly progress to the kitchen with arms out and eyes closed. Completely wrapped in mummy gauze and cobwebs, dust clouds rise as I plop down into a chair at the breakfast table. What IS that smell? Its heavenly perfume wafts through the stale morning air like flowers in springtime. That blissfully delightful aroma is an ancient healing potion, the only thing that breathes fresh life into these dry bones. It is nothing less than a glimmer of hope, a spark of life to this weary soul, coffee.

~ I wish I didn't have to order these IV drip bags and supplies online, it's not my mailman's business how I take my coffee...

~ Here is a great twist on a boring classic, start your kids out right: I'm a little coffee pot short and stout, here is my handle-here is my spout. When I get all brewed up hear me shout, "Tip me over and pour me... ANOTHER cup of that b-e-a-uuuutiful brew right now!"

~ Today started out just like any other day, with potential to be absolutely unforgettable . . . and then I spilled my coffee. It's been completely downhill since... Oh! The horror! Just can't erase the image from my mind... May have to just start over and pour me another...

~ I want to invent a machine about the size of a credit card that would brew fresh, dark, rich coffee. It would sit right on your hip, so thin it is virtually undetectable under clothing. Then, through micro-cell transfer technology, the coffee would just automatically be absorbed right into your body through your skin. ...Then I can ditch the IV pole, and finally, no more messy needles and drip bags to order...

~ Sitting in a Starbucks® Café sipping a delightful caramel macchiato, I watch the ever moving, hustle and bustle of international foot traffic inside the airport. Is there a better way to wait for my children's flight to arrive? I think not.
What's that I hear? Their plane has been delayed?
Oh, rats I may have to order another double shot while I wait...

~ Iced espresso roast blended with sweet Italian cream and a long straw- sipping from a gallon jug cleverly nestled into a baby carrier. Now, adjust the baby carrier so it is at just the right level... and I am ready for that jog around the park. Well saunter, really, with some rest breaks in the shade lounging on a bench under the trees. Even exercise is easier with coffee. So virtually painless, you may not want to call it exercise... Jazzercise was a huge exercise phenomenon– let's start an exercise revolution and call it Javacize.

~ *May this always be your first thought of the day: Yippee! Woo-hoo! Fa-la-la-la.... time to wake up!! Yay!! Hooray!! Be excited! Look, we get another day...what's there not to be happy about? Every day we are gifted is another opportunity to create memorable moments of extraordinary excellence in our lives. Be amazing!! Seek the opportunity to do something completely astonishing today. As a suggestion, start with coffee.*

~ Who keeps drinking my iced coffee? I have had several tall, frosty glasses of my miraculous, magical medicine right here. I turn my back and all of a sudden it's empty...what IS that?? I am telling you, it's coffee gnomes... Believe!!

~ While most roll over and tap their alarm's snooze button on their nightstand, I roll over and without batting an eyelid - hit the "brew" button on my bed side coffee pot... Best alarm on earth, who could dare "snooze" after starting something so amazing, so wonderful?

~ An ingenious idea I intend to share every month...

Dear makers-of-the-chocolate-kiss people:

Will you make a mini kiss (but make it a little more than a peck on the cheek) with a couple espresso beans in it? I imagine smooth, creamy caramel drizzled espresso beans decadently cloaked in dark chocolate. Don't even bother to individually wrap them. Just put them into a large package where I can eat them without even having to use my hands, for fear of gnawing one off.

Sincerely,

Every female coffee lover, ever.

~ *Finishing up my last pot of coffee for the morning. Mmmmmm, a robust and crunchy finish... my favorite! Most folks don't like the grounds in their cup –*
I say, it's coffee, what's there not to love?!

~ I believe we can unite the globe with total and complete coffee love. I don't see coffee love as odd, obsessive, strange or even a little off color. There's nothing more natural than to be so completely head over heels for something that's always there for you, something that makes you feel so good, that lifts you up. Reading this you may think those reasons a bit, dare I call it, selfish. But there are so many other reasons, so much bigger and greater than just myself to absolutely fall unabashedly in love with coffee. On the other side of the globe, a hard working coffee farmer is able to feed his family because of this love. So let's join hands, and love coffee for others, do it for the farmers, for their families, the children, for one coffee love and some day, world coffee love. One love, coffee love.

The Affair

~ Consistency is the key to being successful at anything in life. The only thing I am consistent with at this point in my life, aside from being inconsistent, is my love of coffee. I can't even take credit for that, though – it's just so EASY. Like falling... completely... in love.

~ *The deliciously thick smell of coffee cologne tickles my nose. I sense his mere presence in my home, and it wakes my sleepy eyes... I blink, and breathe in deeply. It is in that moment I realize- I know he's here. The foreign, distant traveler from Pikes Place®- the most perfect Mother's Day morning surprise. I know all too well the pleasures that await just the two of us, and I have every intention to savor every sweet, delectable moment we spend together!*

~ *It's morning, and I am half dressed shuffling into the kitchen to get my coffee. Tapping the spoon on the counter, coffee looked at me expectantly, "Where have you been, we are almost late for work!" Unable to make eye contact, I sheepishly replied, "I've been with the bed..." Heated and jealous words were exchanged. A word to the wise, don't be afraid to stand your ground, the best part of the argument – is the making up...*

~ *Humming to myself as I go through my morning ritual with mascara wand in hand, a deep, soothing voice from behind me asks, "Hey Baby... Did you do something different with your hair? You look so nice this morning." I was taken by surprise, and turned towards the voice. There he was, and I saw him- dark, rich, handsome- standing so close and leaning over me against the bathroom door. His dreamy gaze met mine, and he flashed an irresistible smile. He took my breath away, and my goodness – smelled so good. I breathed him in... "Coffee," I gasped, "Where have you been? I have been waiting for you". He leaned even closer to me; I felt his steamy breath caress my neck. "I was in the kitchen". He is so captivating, so tantalizing this morning – I may just have to call in sick to work.*

~ Looking back, it was obvious. "You're spending too much time with that iPod®, what does he have, that I don't have? What do you see in that thing?" Coffee was jealously interrogating me... Heartbroken, I recently discovered my iPod® lying lifeless at the bottom of my purse with dried coffee marks all over it. Is this a coincidence? I think not!

~ I am not sure if it was a midlife crisis, or just a desire for a little more spontaneity- but I recently switched from my regular roast to Italian roast for about a week now. Suddenly I'm talking with my hands, I feel powerful and confident – kinda like a mob boss... I am longing to travel the fields of Italy, wear fancy Italian shoes... I find myself adding pesto and tomato sauce to all my food, and what's even more disturbing? I have seemingly picked up an Italian accent. What's a matter for me, uh!?

~ You are the first thing I think of when my sleepy eyes wake in the morning. I am laughing to myself when I think of the funny things you say – I dance around the house in the mornings and I can't wait to see you again ... Thank you coffee for making my life so much better because you are in it!

22

~ *Recently I had tried to do an ancestry search on the internet. All the leads proved to be dead ends. Determined to get to the bottom of it, I contacted my mother. We shared a cup of coffee in an undisclosed location. The conversation was meaningful, candid and very open. I had so many unanswered questions. Under the pressure of such an encounter, and much to my surprise, my mother admitted that I was the illegitimate love-child from a long standing affair she's had with coffee... And in that moment, there was clarity, it is all falling into place now...*

~ *My coffee reminds me of Antonio Banderas today...*

he thinks the Zorro mask is silly

but I like it!

~ *I pushed down the half-moon shaped plastic top that stood between me and the "For Emergency Only" powdered coffee creamer, and I realized something... The half-moon shape that pushes in on the top to open the canister looks like the mouth of a winking, one-eyed smiley face! Now, not only does my coffee have a drop dead gorgeous smile, but the emergency powdered creamer too!!*

Oh myyy....

~ *Java Jive:*

Every morning,	*When I wake in the night*	*Coffee, it's too long to*
My heart's a buzz	*From a terrible dream,*	*Wait all night for a kiss.*
You're first on my mind	*I run to the kitchen*	*Baby, you're my coffee*
My one true love.	*Pour some coffee and cream.*	*And I'm your girl,*
Like the feeling you get	*I must be with you*	*There's no love like you*
When life's complete,	*Or I'm feeling amiss*	*In this whole wide world!*
Its all bout you,		
I can't even sleep.		

24

~ The soft rain falls all around us as coffee's gaze meets mine. I lean back against the aged trunk of this mighty oak that canopies us from the storm and he flashes that smile that melts the edges off every one of my thoughts and feelings. How could I be mad that he dragged me out here for a romantic walk in the woods, too far to walk back home in the rain... I am so in love with this coffee... There's something so purely romantic about getting caught out here in this rainstorm – and as his lips met mine, I secretly hoped it would rain all day.

~ Oh coffee, your sweet goodness ignites a fire in my belly and lights up my soul like the twinkling stars in the deepest heavens. My first sip this morning was nothing less than luscious and tantalizing, like the first seductive kiss from a long lost lover.

~ Sleepily lying enveloped in masked and velvet-caped coffee fantasies, where my sweet love, the brave and dashing espresso roast draws his mighty sword and swoops in to rescue me just as the sandman put his sleeper hold on me. He then whisks me away in his safe and strong arms and I smile, even though I know my handsome hero exists only in my dreams.

~ Sometimes I run a little behind in the morning. How can I help it, with sweet fairy tale endings woven into my early morning daydreams followed up with serious make out sessions with my coffee cup that may last a little too long? Time flies when you are kissing coffee... but it's the perfect start to every day!

~ Tall wheat fields make the perfect cover for my coffee lover and me to lie together on a soft blanket in hiding. I love how the sun warms our skin as it shines down from the perfect sapphire sky. We laugh and kiss, entwined together as we spend the lazy afternoon watching cloud animals smile and wave as they pass us by...

~ Lying in bed, snuggled up in my fleece coffee blanket and my super soft tee shirt sheets. I can hear whispers and giggles coming from the kitchen and sneaking down the hall. Oh, silly coffeepot, we both know sleep is overrated but I will see you in the morning!

~ Sharing a candlelit dinner together, coffee's heart speaks to mine and I feel it skip a beat. Every touch, every smile, drives me crazy – your caress takes me right to the brink. I take a deep breath, afraid I will cause a scene. I must maintain my composure, but I cannot wait – tonight is the night we share our first kiss. I can feel it in my bones – tonight is the night. And as we share funny stories and colorful conversation I can tell from that look in your eyes, you feel the same. After dinner you ask what I want for dessert, and I am speechless – we both bust out laughing because we were thinking about the exact same thing. Nobody else gets me like you do, coffee – and I love you for it!

~ I long to hear the romantic whispers of my foreign lover, everywhere I turn, he is there... Je t'aime ... whispered in the kitchen. ... Je t'aime ... I hear it behind me in the hall ... Je t'aime ... I cannot fathom life and love before meeting that romantic French roast coffee. I am already planning our next romantic encounter. After a candle lit cup together, I plan to have my way with him. I will devour every last bit of him and what's even more romantic? He doesn't speak a word of English...

~ I am completely entranced by you, your sweet taste lingering on my tongue...the way you softly kiss my lips, the immediate passion... our eyes meet and we are entwined together in this, the perfect affair. Breathless, I sit alone at the table – remembering our time together. I take my last sip of deep decadence and you are gone, the memory of us together lingers... Coffee, we belong together...

~ Driving down the road with the top down and breeze blowing through our hair; coffee, smiling, rides shotgun. This is our favorite type of romantic trip to take together. There is no map, no plan, no destination – just two amorous and free spirits out for a weekend adventure on a beautiful afternoon. Neither of us knows where we will end up, but we both know the night will end in each others arms.

~ Together we sit in the sand; the beach stretches out for miles in both directions. A fresh breeze cools us as the soft, gentle waves lick at our little toes. Coffee slips out a tiny giggle and it makes me laugh- how real, how shameless he is. In an effort to quickly divert attention, he flashes that killer smile and glances at me over the top of his sunglasses. He pauses a moment and then says to me, "I can't get over how sexy you look right now." ...and I am sure it wasn't the sun kissing my cheeks that made me turn so red. I couldn't help but think to myself, "Yes, shameless indeed... but somehow I think I will manage."

~ Took a long walk down a country dirt road, hand in hand, the incredible color bursts of fall surround us entirely. Crimson leaves overhead, brilliant gold and burnt oranges frame our path as our shoes crunched the road beneath us. The crisp smell of fall is in the air. Coffee was so adorable in his little red and black plaid fleece shirt. My favorite part was when he carved our initials in a heart on the old oak tree at the top of the hill, I was certain I had stepped right off the set of a romantic fairy tale movie.

~ Today started out like any other, until that sweet little French roast began to serenade me over coffee. I can still hear him singing his little heart out to me. It felt like we were the only two in the whole world and time stood completely still the moment he looked into my eyes- and all I could do is blush. And sip my coffee, of course.

~ I was thinking about immortalizing my love for coffee in the form of a tattoo. Nothing says "true love forever" like a little permanent ink. So I was contemplating what image to choose when the simple coffee bean entered my mind – so much symbolism, the color of the earth which all life comes from and returns to, the bean is a complete oval with no beginning and no end just like infinity. Then I thought about what it would look like by the time I got to a nursing home and it didn't matter where I put it – eventually gravity would pull that thing from a artistically depicted pile of beautiful coffee beans into a neat looking pile of poo. I opted for a bumper sticker instead.

~ We sit quietly together, by candlelight, enjoying the peacefulness of the gentle night sounds; coffee is snuggled into the love seat next to me. I feel a gentle brush on my arm and turn to see that far away look in his eyes, and sense his serenity while looking into the night sky. His gaze slowly meets mine, and all around the fireflies light the darkness that envelops us. Above us, the stars wink and twinkle to one other, silently spelling out the rest of our love story.

The Essence of Life

~ Everybody has done it – had a bad idea that seemed like a good one at the time. It's early morning and I had decided I was going to reorganize and stock my bathroom. I don't know why, don't ask me. I remember trying to work quickly and efficiently, but feeling like something was a little "off". As I tossed the rolls of toilet paper across the room to restock the bathroom, I knew it was a bad idea. Just as the rolls left my fingertips I realized due to my dulled senses and lack of foresight this morning I was inadvertently toilet papering the inside of my house...

New rule #1: Touch nothing prior to the coffee pot.

~ In deep, sleepy, night-time dreams, I was wrapped snugly in the arms of a loving octopus (much to my chagrin). As the darkness let loose its grip on me and the morning crested in my consciousness I realized my warped reality... I was twisted in the heating blanket, getting a tongue bath from the dog...the only thing that can make any of this right is a smooth and immediate make out session with a near by coffee cup. STAT!

~ Was in bed by 7:30, slept straight thru till morning- does that make me "old"? Maybe. Whether I accept the fact that I am old or not, the older generation is by far the most dedicated of all coffee lovers. Some cannot remember who they are, where they are, if they have been married or whether they have children without being prompted to remember – but ask how they take their coffee and there is not a one that cannot tell you. How can such a love transcend life itself? Millions of our elders can't be wrong!

~ At work sitting desk side, sipping my magical bean elixir and plotting out my plan for the day...I love that my job is to truly make a difference in people's lives! I know this coffee is making a difference in mine!

~ So there I was, lying there, sound asleep snuggled into the electric blanket dreaming about something happy. Before I know it, the pesky alarm is summoning me to get up. What time is it anyway!? Hard as I might- despite trying again and again, I just absolutely cannot see the alarm clock ...and then I realize, I need to open my eyes first. That's when the sudden realization sunk in that all my circuits run on coffee and this tank was trying to run on empty. Never again!

~ As a general rule of thumb I try not to give advice, but in this case I am going to give you a heads up: Avoid the vente triple espresso shot, cherry mocha Frappuccino® after 10 pm... Unless, of course, you are hopelessly desperate to not sleep all night! This may work to the advantage of many... College kids, teenagers, third shift working crews and all insomniacs everywhere, UNITE!

~ Tapping the Espresso roast, Italian roast and Sumatra® coffee packages where their little belly buttons should be, I recited the elementary school solution for choosing between the things you love. "Eeny meeney miney moe, catch my coffee by the toe"... In the end the determining finger landed squarely on the belly of my little buddy Espresso roast. As I opened the bag to fill the awaiting filter, I swear I heard a giggle squeak out of the bag...

~ I like my coffee super strong, almost chewable. I am wondering if it can get any stronger – I am trying to upgrade my natural moon-kissed complexion to a somewhat of a more olive-tan glow from the inside out. I really think I might be on to something...

~ I have been thinking all year about this and I have decided these are the three wishes I would like granted for my birthday:

<u>Wish #1</u>: I wish for my mail person to weed out all the bills from the mail and save them for the day after my birthday.

<u>Wish #2</u>: That rainbows would follow me wherever I go. That would be cool. People would say, "Did you see that rainbow driving down the street?" And I would just chuckle because I know it was my rainbow.

Now, the best for last.

<u>My wish #3</u>: I could get a cup of Starbucks® without having to drive a minimum of 46 minutes one way if the traffic is just right, to get it. There are Starbucks® across the street from Starbucks® in this country, how can this be right? **tucks wishes under pillow** I will let you know what happens.

~ When the weather gets warm,
I love iced coffee. I watch the
condensation drip down the glass of
coffee, as ice cubes drift in dark and
decadent coffee splashed with cream.
Everything is right in the world. I
close my eyes and listen... The bird's
chirping blends with the sound of the
clinking ice cubes in my glass, and it
all melds into a sweet and wonderful
morning song. What's equally as
beautiful is the way it magically
disappears into my belly.

~**Disco ball drops from the kitchen ceiling and rotates above the coffee pot, the lights dim and music plays** Today I am motivated by the rhythm of disco and fueled by the power of pure coffee! It's a java Flashdance Celebration, and I Will Survive! Coffee is my Macho Man and I will be coffee's Dancing Queen in Funkytown... Oh coffee, Ring My Bell, Play That Funky Music and Shake Shake Shake that booty like you're at the YMCA! 'Cause coffee, I Need Your Lovin'!

~ Sometimes I think I am really just a tiny person inside my brain sitting in an elaborate control room, looking out the holes in my head where my eyeballs are. I am sipping a tiny thimbleful of coffee, and kicking back in the black leather office chair with my feet up on the control center counter...

~ I think any official or government form that asks your name, address, birthday, sex and social security number should also include a box that says "Coffee Y/N" because, yes, it is just that important.

~ I am laying in bed, counting coffee cups to lure in my sleep. Closing my eyes, I dream of the beautiful chocolaty color of that deep, rich, bold coffee which has yet to be born- but is destined to fill my cup in the morning!

~ There's nothing better after a long, hard work day than a foofey, poufy bubble bath piled high with sparkling bubbles, coupled with a polka dotted coffee mug filled to the rim with Starbucks® Gazebo Blend...hmmm... Or maybe a better scenario would be to just dump the coffee pot into the tub, and climb in for a dip and ignite an evening of sultry yet delightful indulgence...

~ Sometimes doing good things for your health isn't always easy but drinking coffee is always an easy choice. Coffee comes from beans; most beans are supposed to be some kind of protein, so that's good. Cocoa beans have antioxidants so naturally coffee probably does too. And if you happen to drink a few grounds when you kick back your last swig from the cup well, that's just that extra fiber everyone's raving about. Let's not forget that our bodies need water, and that's how coffee is brewed. Who could argue? It's just so good! AND good for you! Bottoms up!

~ Yes, the amount of force that exits a blow dryer IS strong enough to blow any hot or cool liquid from an open topped glass, even while you are actually drinking out of it. The experiment was ingenious, just wish I could take credit for actually planning and trying out that theory on purpose...

~ Ever have a day where you wake up, and all the colors in the sky are different, and no matter what happens- nobody is going to get you down? Purpose to make today your day. Take it, seize the day – you have the power. If, somehow, you have managed to read this before your first sip of coffee, just think – it's about to get even better!

~ At the mall with my mother, and something shiny catches her attention and before I know it I am stranded in a sea of people busily scurrying about. I didn't have to look far, before I managed to find safe harbor, heaven on earth, calm in the storm- a Starbucks®! Hmmm... think I will order a double shot caramel macchiato and get a private table in the back, there's about to be a serious public display of affection!

~ The stakes are too high; the risk of bodily injury is imminent if I attempt to function as a real person without my morning coffee. I snoozed this morning just long enough for the coffee pot to work its magic – what's the point of even getting up to sit on the edge of the bed if the coffee isn't ready yet? With my record for klutziness, I may pull an ovary just trying to kick off my blankets.

~ Drowsy and lethargic I find myself driving through the morning mist, the tranquil earth still blanketed by the darkness of night. I feel like a lost sailor on the open seas looking for safe harbor. Ahead I see a dim beacon of light in the stillness, and as I draw near to the source of this light I realize that not only have I found safe harbor, but a little piece of paradise on earth, an open and operating Starbucks®.

~ *My secret plight to coffee creamer companies:*

Dear people that make the packaging for coffee creamer;

You know that little foil seal you super glue with gorilla elephant glue for "safety", has anyone ever considered the fact that there is a possibility it may be near impossible for anyone to get that thing off in the morning considering they haven't had their coffee yet!? I am an able bodied adult, but to try to coordinate the iron fisted two finger pinch needed to pull that stupid little thing off before I even have my eyes open yet is just too much to ask. Please consider a safe and user friendly alternative like the full palmed handle, much like a rip cord you would find on parachute.

THANK YOU!!!!!!!!!!!!!!!!!!!!!!!!

Signed,

An uncoordinated, early morning coffee drinker

~ *The moment I realized I put my pants on backwards again this morning I decided to kill two birds with one stone. I had a big, wholesome bowl of fresh ground espresso roast with a splash of milk this morning for breakfast. Reminds me of Grape Nuts®, but plugged into a nuclear power plant!*

~ *Who else thinks coffee could pass as it's own food group?*

~ With Starbucks® pumping through my system, I have a little extra energy this morning. Singing into my coffee cup, I am dancing around and shaking it in the kitchen to my favorite groovalicious disco jam... I strike a pose over the vent on the floor, and right on cue the furnace kicks on and blows my hair back with meticulous movie star timing. Yeah, it's going to be a great day!

~ So psyched for the day, just hope the world is ready for me. I'm kicking butt and taking names fueled by the perfect goodness of coffee!

Coffee ninjas UNITE!

~ Someone recently told me I didn't look my age; and wanted to know "my secret" to looking young. Well, my nutrition drink of choice is coffee, my favorite exercise is laughing, and my favorite past time is sleeping. There, now the secret to agelessness is out. Love, Laugh, Dream.

~ Initially I was horrified the day I stepped into the kitchen and saw the coffee pot had some type of hot clear liquid in it. WHERE'S MY COFFEE?? My theory is the coffee gnomes emptied the grounds out of the filter the night before. I dumped a scoop of fresh ground coffee into my hot water and drank it down, that'll show those little gnomes!

~ Enjoying a hot cup of Starbucks® Anniversary blend this morning and I am flashing back to a time and a place when I lived in the middle of a modern day civilization, where you could just walk down the block and order a hot cup of luxurious magnificence and so many more delightful treats any time your little heart desired. In my area, you could opt for gas station "coffee" or head to the local coffee shop which opens at 10 am. It's all just so wrong... Be this a lesson to those within the sound of this book, and within a stones throw from a Starbucks® - never, never, never take good coffee for granted!

~ Woke up this morning, and in my imagination John Mayer was performing a private concert in my kitchen. Holding my cup of espresso roast as I watched him swaying in front of the microphone, strumming his guitar and singing my favorite song, I wondered if my imagination made me blessed, or crazy. Then he winked at me and I think we both knew the answer to that question...

~ Sometimes I am at work before my coffee kicks in. As the Jamaican blue mountain coffee roused my neurons on a cellular level, I realized not only were my pants on inside out, but backwards as well. How many people have noticed this before me? Seriously, I really need to start my first cup before I even open my eyes some days, honestly!

~ I am inspired! I am inspired to do better, to be better, to move faster, run farther, laugh harder and chase my dreams to the end of the earth and back. Oh, oops, wait a minute... There, now I have my coffee – now, I can believe it! Get your coffee and be inspired!

~ True happiness begins deep within each of us. I feel love, joy and true happiness radiating out from that warm spot deep in my tummy where my first sip of coffee rests. I close my eyes, and meditate on that feeling – over time, coffee has become my happy place, where love, peace and joy reside. Feel the love and pass it on!

~ Seems my value of a good pot of coffee is shared by at least one of my co workers. Her exact words were, "One cup of coffee isn't enough to do much. Sure, one cup will open your eyes, but it won't make you spry!" Well said, my friend!

~ Shaking two bottles of coffee creamer like maracas in the kitchen on my way from the fridge to the coffeepot all the while dancing and shaking it. I was doing my spirited impression of an improvised salsa... for my big finish I slide the last few feet on the floor towards the counter (arms up over my head while sort-of doing the splits with absolutely no fore thought as to how I was going to get up off the floor), and out of the corner of my eye I actually saw both of my dogs roll their eyes at me.

~ With technology advancing every day, it is completely possible to share a cup of coffee with someone who isn't even on your continent. It doesn't matter if you don't speak the language – we are all bonded by our love of coffee, and a smile is its own internationally recognized language. One world, one love, coffee love!

~ As I lay here counting popcorn texture bumps on the ceiling I notice a soft, familiar glow from behind my alarm clock. As I peer over the top of the clock, I see the tooth fairy and the sandman chatting together, sitting on the edge of the night stand having a cup of coffee. Guess the night's just beginning for all of us...

~ In this experience we call life, I am skinny dipping in the pool of a delectable coffee culture – so please, don't throw me a life jacket!!

33701000R00035

Made in the USA
Lexington, KY
05 July 2014